key to re

At Key Porter Kids, we understand how important reading is to a young child's development. That's why we created the Key to Reading program, a structured approach to reading for the beginner. While the books in this series are educational, they are also engaging and fun — key elements in gaining and retaining a child's interest. Plus, with each level in the program designed for different reading abilities, children can advance at their own pace and become successful, confident readers in the process.

Level 1: The Beginner
For children familiar with the alphabet and ready to begin reading.
- Very large type
- Simple words
- Short sentences
- Repetition of key words
- Picture cues
- Colour associations
- Directional reading
- Picture match-up cards

Level 2: The Emerging Reader
For children able to recognize familiar words on sight and sound out new words with help.
- Large type
- Easy words
- Longer sentences
- Repetition of key words and phrases
- Picture cues
- Context cues
- Directional reading
- Picture and word match-up cards

Level 3: The Independent Reader
For increasingly confident readers who can sound out new words on their own.
- Large type
- Expanded vocabulary
- Longer sentences and paragraphs
- Repetition of longer words and phrases
- Picture cues
- Context cues
- More complex storylines
- Flash cards

Max was playing fireman.
He wore a red fireman's hat.
He played with a red fire truck.

"Fireman!" said Max.
The fire truck drove away.

Ruby was skipping with Louise.
Ruby jumped and counted.
"One…"

4

The fire truck drove under Ruby.
"Max," said Ruby.
"Please play somewhere else."

Max played with the white hose.
It was short.

Max found a green hose.
It was long.
"Fireman!" said Max.

Ruby started to skip again.
"One..."

Max bumped into Ruby.
"Max," said Ruby.
"Please play somewhere else."

Max played with the yellow ladder.
It was small.

Max found another ladder.
It was tall.
"Fireman!" said Max.

Ruby started to skip again.
"One..."

Max bumped into Louise.
"Max," said Ruby.
"Please play somewhere else."

Max played with the toys
in the sandbox.
They all drove away!

**Bunny Scout Leader came
to watch Ruby.
Ruby got ready to skip.**

The red fire truck
drove toward Ruby.
Ruby skipped: "One!"

**The white ambulance
drove toward Ruby.
Ruby skipped again: "Two!"**

The black and white police car
drove toward Ruby.
Ruby skipped again: "Three!"

"What a special skipping game,"
said Bunny Scout Leader.
"What do you call it?"

"Fireman!" said Max.

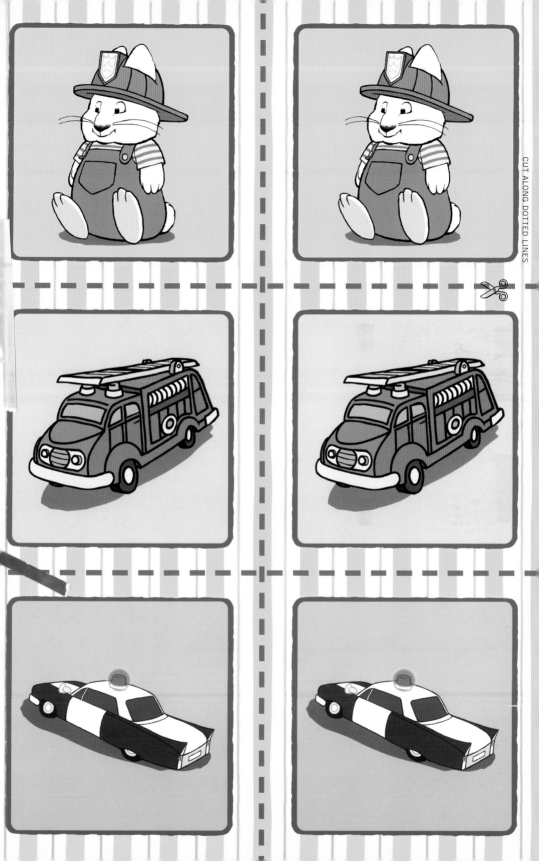